ADVENTURES of the

Steampunk PiRates

The Leaky Battery
Sets Sail

To Captain Jacob & First Mate Ella Leggett – GPJ

To Mr Alden, my geography teacher, for his
encouragement and fashion sense – FAD

STRIPES PUBLISHING
An imprint of Little Tiger Press
1 The Coda Centre, 189 Munster Road,
London SW6 6AW

A paperback original
First published in Great Britain in 2015

ISBN: 978-1-84715-593-1

A CIP catalogue record for this book is available
from the British Library.

Printed and bound in the UK.

10 9 8 7 6 5 4 3 2 1

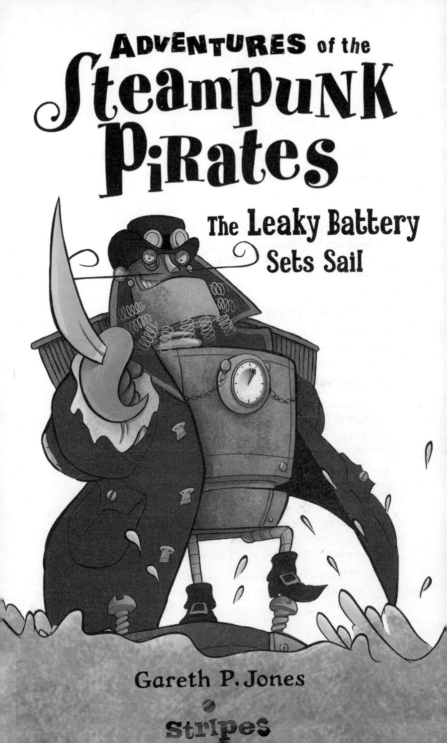

ADVENTURES of the
Steampunk
Pirates

The Leaky Battery Sets Sail

Gareth P. Jones

Stripes

WANTED

DEAD OR ALIVE!

(or smashed into little bits and delivered in boxes)

The crew of the *Leaky Battery* the STEAMPUNK PIRATES for piracy, looting and treason.

Sixteen scurrilous scallywags in total, including their four officers:

CAPTAIN CLOCKHEART
Hot-headed leader of the Steampunk Pirates. He is unpredictable and dangerous on account of a loose valve sending too much steam to his head.

FIRST MATE MAINSPRING
Operated by clockwork, he is at his most dangerous when overly wound up.

QUARTERMASTER LEXI
Fitted with a catalogue of information, he is the cleverest (if not the bravest) of the bunch.

MR GADGE
His various arm attachments include all kinds of devilish weaponry and fighting equipment.

A REWARD OF
ONE THOUSAND POUNDS
is offered for anyone who captures this crew of loathsome looters and returns them to their rightful owner, the King of England.

We are the Steampunk Pirates,
We're fearless, brave and bold,
If you care to listen,
Our story will unfold,
With fire in our bellies,
We're here to steal your gold,
We're rough and tough,
We'll take your stuff,
And we won't do what we're told
(We're told!)
We won't do what we're told!

CHAPTER 1

In which our heroes,
the Steampunk Pirates, attack the
HMS Regency, and its commander,
Admiral Fussington, demonstrates
how, when it comes to surrendering,
the English are second to none.

At first glance, there was nothing especially remarkable about the pirate ship that emerged from the thick sea mist and drew alongside the *HMS Regency*. Its billowing sails were white. Its flapping flag was black. Its crew of ragged buccaneers jeered and cheered and waved their razor-sharp

cutlasses as their captain cried, "Surrender, you English mummy's boys or we'll fire up the cannons and blast more holes in your ship than you'll find in a barrel full of Dutch cheese, so we will."

However, these were no ordinary pirates. Under the captain's dark blue hat was a face made of metal that glinted in the sunlight. Steam shot out of his ears and his head. He wore a heavy woollen coat, open at the front to reveal a clock on his chest. It had only one hand that was madly whizzing around.

"Oh no, it's the *Leaky Battery*!" cried the terrified lookout on the *HMS Regency*. "It's Captain Clockheart and the Steampunk Pirates!"

Captain Clockheart laughed. "You hear

that, First Mate Mainspring? Load up the cannons."

"**Click**, aye. **Tick**, aye. **Tock**, Captain," replied a pirate with a bowler hat, chequered trousers and a large key slowly rotating in the middle of his back.

"We surrender!" Admiral Fussington immediately raised his hands.

"Load 'em up and prepare to… Hold on. Did you say *surrender*?"

"Yes! Don't fire – we give up." Admiral Fussington turned to his crew. "Sergeant Thudchump, order your soldiers to lower their weapons."

The sergeant motioned to the rest of the crew and they reluctantly put down their guns.

The hand on the captain's clock suddenly

stopped and steam *put-put-putted* out of his head in confusion. "I don't understand."

"Och. Let's blast 'em to smithereens. Surrendering is no way to stop us attacking," snarled Mr Gadge, who wore a tartan kilt and bandana to match, and had a hook in place of his left hand. He twisted his arm and the hook was replaced with a cannon ramrod.

"Hold your fire, Gadge," said the captain. "I'd like to know why a ship of the Royal Navy would surrender so quickly."

A mechanical bird with a few colourful feathers glued to

its wings landed on his shoulder and squawked, "A bunch of scaredy cats!"

"How rude. Not at all," protested Admiral Fussington. "I'm simply following the latest guidelines with regards to P.C.S.s."

"Ah, ignore Twitter," said Captain Clockheart. "What's a P.C.S. when it's at home?"

"A potential conflict situation. The rules now state that senior officers should immediately surrender. Look, I've got a kit and everything." The admiral opened a bag and pulled out a stick with a white flag wrapped around it. After carefully reading the instructions, he unfurled the flag and gave it a little wave.

Captain Clockheart laughed then turned to the rest of his crew, who joined in, their

mechanical jaws clanking and clinking.

"Right, you lot," yelled the captain.
"First Mate Mainspring, lower the boarding
planks. Gadge, Loose-screw, Blind Bob
Bolt and the rest of you merciless metallic
marauders ... PREPARE TO BOARD!"

Gadge fired a grappling hook at the

neighbouring ship's main sail and all the pirates cheered. All except for one, who wore a frilly shirt and had a device at the top of his head, which sent small bits of paper flitting around, making a fluttering sound as they turned.

"Ahem, if I may have a word, sir."

"What is it, Quartermaster Lexi?" snapped Captain Clockheart, the vapour from his head twisting up like a mini-tornado.

"I'm not sure that boarding this vessel is altogether a good idea," he replied anxiously.

"Spoil sport! Spoil sport!" squawked Twitter.

"Quite right," said Captain Clockheart.

"That's not fair," protested Lexi. "I'm just saying that the chances of this being—"

Captain Clockheart banged the back of Lexi's head and the quartermaster instantly went quiet and stopped moving. "That's better. There's a good reason why the only one of us with any brains has an off switch." He laughed. "Piracy's not about thinking or worrying – it's about taking what you can!"

14

The captain's clock hand began to move quickly again and he cried, "Now, you horrible lot, all aboard this ship before I send you to the sharks for dillying and dallying. Take all the gold and coal you can find."

The crew of the *Leaky Battery* lowered the boarding planks and made their way over to the *HMS Regency*, where the smartly dressed naval officers stood with their raised hands shaking in fear.

"Search the ship," ordered Captain Clockheart.

"Yes. Take whatever you need," said Admiral Fussington, who was still waving his white flag.

"I like this new policy of yours, Admiral," said Captain Clockheart. "Now, would you be so kind as to empty your pockets and hand over your ... GOLD." The steam shot excitedly from the pirate's nostrils as he said the word.

The admiral pulled out a small purse. "This is all the money I have," he said.

Captain Clockheart emptied the coins into his palm and tested one between his metal teeth.

"Do you ... eat metal?" asked the admiral, looking equally intrigued and appalled.

"Eat it?" said Captain Clockheart, with a low chuckle. "No, we don't eat it. The fire in our bellies requires coal and wood."

"Then what do you want with it?"

"Let me show you." Captain Clockheart pulled back his sleeve to reveal that his wrist was made of gold. "I saved up my booty from the last three raids to make this beauty."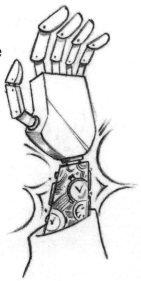

"Why would you want gold body parts?"

"Because our maker saw fit to craft us from iron, a metal that rusts. The salt water eats away at our parts something horrible. And there's nothing more painful than rusty nuts and bolts, I can tell you. We don't wear these rags for comfort,

warmth or modesty. We need to protect our metal from the elements, so we do."

"But there are other metals that don't rust…" the admiral pointed out. "Copper or silver are easier to find than gold."

"Ah, but nothing *feels* like gold," said Captain Clockheart. "A soft-skinned landlubber like you wouldn't understand. Gold is the finest of all metals and, one day, I'll have more than a gold wrist. One day, this entire ship will glisten with golden glory. Then maybe we'll give up this pirating lark for good. But until then … hand over your booty."

The author of this work apologizes for this interruption, but he wonders if you, the reader, might like to learn how the Steampunk Pirates were created.

Penelope, daughter of Admiral Fussington, had been fascinated by the world of engineering ever since her first trip on a steam train but, since it was not considered a suitable subject for a young lady, she had worked in secret on her own steam-powered project.

After several weeks of furtive hammering,

welding and forging, Penelope succeeded in creating a steam-powered bird, capable of flight and basic word repetition. She named it Twitter.

She was proud of her creation and keen to show it to someone who would understand what she had done. When she heard that the famous inventor, Mr Richmond Swift, would be unveiling his latest creation at the king's birthday party, she begged her parents to allow her to go.

Penelope arrived at the palace with a ribbon in her hair, a pretty blue dress and a mechanical bird hidden in her purse. She hastily lost her parents, who just as quickly forgot about her, and went in search of Mr Swift.

The inventor looked exactly as Penelope

had imagined. He had a head of wild white hair, wispy sideburns and excitable eyes.

"Mr Swift, sir," she said. "My name is Penelope and one day I want to be an inventor just like you."

The famous inventor looked her up and down, then laughed. "Very amusing," he said. "Very amusing indeed. Who put you up to this? Was it that joker, the Prince of Wales?"

"No one put me up to anything! I even have my own steam-powered invention to show you."

Penelope went to open her bag but Mr Richmond Swift had already turned away.

"Please step aside, young lady. I have

an announcement to make." He clapped his hands. "Ladies and gentleman, Your Royal Highness. As a birthday present for His Majesty, the king, I have created a brand-new form of serving device that will revolutionize life as we know it. I present ... the Steampunk Servants."

The guests watched, open-mouthed, as sixteen metal robots of different shapes and sizes entered the grand hall, carrying trays of drinks and nibbles.

"It's a trick," said a balding lord. "I'll wager there are children inside."

"Not at all. These are powered by fire and water," said Mr Swift. "No child could withstand such heat." The inventor opened a panel in one of the servant's bellies and revealed the roaring fire within.

"Quite remarkable," said the king.

"I notice that they are not all the same," said a low-ranking member of the royal family with a chin the size of a diving board.

"That is true. There are a dozen basic servants, capable of following instructions, and four with more sophisticated skills. Mr Mainspring here runs on clockwork rather than steam." Mr Swift pointed to one with

a key in its back. "Whereas Mr Gadge has many attachments that will prove useful in the kitchen and the garden."

The servant demonstrated this by turning his arm and switching his hand from a meat fork to a scrubbing brush.

"Why isn't this one carrying a tray?" asked a lady in a large purple dress that made her look like an overly fussy sponge cake.

"Mr Clockheart is the head butler. The others are designed to follow his orders."

The purple sponge lady peered at the peculiar mechanical man. "How can a machine give orders?"

"Allow me." Mr Swift nudged her aside and said, "Mr Clockheart, what is your purpose?"

"We must assist," said the servant in a

flat, robotic voice. "We must assist."

Everyone gasped and several ladies fainted.

"How is this possible?" asked the king.

"Basic speech is little more than a series of sounds put together to express meaning. These machines are able to copy the sounds they hear," replied Mr Swift. "But, rest assured, they do not have the ability to think for themselves. Well, all except for Master Lexi here. This roller-deck device enables him to look up dictionary definitions, encyclopedia entries and suchlike."

"Intriguing," said the king. "Tell me, then, Master Lexi, do you know who I am?"

The wheel in his head whirred and clicked and Lexi responded, "You are King William the fourth, ruler of the United Kingdom and the British Empire." He saluted, raising a

laugh from some of the crowd.

"They certainly seem a good deal less insolent than my servants," said the big-chinned man.

"I daresay they ask for less money, too," agreed his wife. "Cheap labour is terribly expensive these days."

"Servants are like horses," said a duchess, who looked a little like a horse herself. She snatched a large piece of pastry from a tray and shoved it into her mouth. "It is important to let them know who is in charge," she said, spraying out bits of food.

"Well, Mr Swift, it is a remarkable achievement," said the king. "Do help yourself to a knighthood on the way out."

Mr Swift bowed graciously. "Thank you, Your Majesty."

"Steam-powered men?" said an archbishop with a large belly. "It goes against the very principles of nature."

"Never mind that," said a toffee-nosed count. "These fellows have run out of drinks."

Mr Richmond Swift clapped his hands together. "Mr Clockheart, take the others back to the kitchen to refill their trays."

"We will assist."

The mechanical servants left. The party guests carried on chatting and laughing and gossiping. No one noticed that the spirited young daughter of Admiral Fussington had followed them into the kitchen.

The author apologizes for interrupting this interruption but something rather exciting is about to happen in the story.

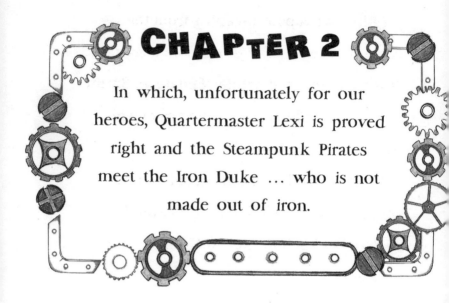

CHAPTER 2

In which, unfortunately for our heroes, Quartermaster Lexi is proved right and the Steampunk Pirates meet the Iron Duke ... who is not made out of iron.

With the tip of his cutlass, Captain Clockheart tugged on a chain around Admiral Fussington's neck and pulled out a small, gold, heart-shaped pendant.

"Ah, Admiral," he said, inspecting the item. "It seems you have a heart of gold."

The admiral coughed and wafted away

the cloud of vapour escaping from the captain. "Please don't take it," he begged. "It's a gift for my daughter, Penelope. Surely even you wouldn't rob a little girl of a gift from her doting father."

"You can't rob someone of something they never had," shouted Pendle, the *Leaky Battery*'s cabin boy, the only human crew member.

"Pendle lad," said Captain Clockheart, "I've told you before – cabin boys have no place on ship raids."

"I say … you look familiar, lad." Admiral Fussington peered suspiciously at Pendle. "What's the name of your father?"

The boy saluted Captain Clockheart and scurried off, ignoring the admiral.

"I'll be asking the questions," said Captain Clockheart. "Now, hand over your gold heart before I make a hole in your regular one."

"I worked hard to earn enough to buy this gift," protested the admiral.

"I'll say. Gold this fine don't come cheap."

"Actually, if you must know, I couldn't afford to buy a gold one. This was silver till I had it converted."

"Converted?" said Captain Clockheart.

"What does that mean?"

"Converted," said Lexi, his word-wheel starting up again. "Changed, altered, transformed."

"Oh, you're back on again, are you?" sighed the captain.

"I am. And I have to say, I find it most objectionable that you can switch me off whenever you please," said Lexi.

"Never mind that," said Captain Clockheart. "How can silver be turned into gold, Admiral?"

Admiral Fussington explained. "I met an American gentleman by the name of Chas Goldman, who has mastered the ancient art of alchemy."

"What?" demanded Captain Clockheart.

"Alchemy is a form of science in which

base metals are turned into gold," said Quartermaster Lexi, his word-wheel whirring. "Although I can find no record of it ever being achieved."

"Why have I never heard of this?"

"Perhaps if you spent more time reading and less time bashing people on the head, you would have," said Lexi pointedly.

The captain turned back to the admiral. "Where can I find this Goldman chap?"

"He lives on Snake Island. It's one of the Too Many Islands, just south-west of here."

"Fascinating," said Lexi, "but as I was saying, Captain, before you so rudely switched me off, there is a strong possibility that this whole thing is a trap."

Captain Clockheart's laughter sent little gassy bursts shooting out from every part

of his head. "A trap, Lexi? We're plundering this ship good and proper. What kind of trap would it be?"

"One that has been brilliantly executed … just as you will be."

The captain whirled around to see who had spoken. It was a man with ruddy cheeks, a scarlet jacket adorned with shiny medals and a victorious look in his dark eyes.

He was standing on a huge warship that had appeared out of the dense sea mist. It towered over the *Leaky Battery*.

"It's a trap! It's a trap!" squawked Twitter.

Two more ships loomed out of the mist.

"**Click**, Clockheart, you fool," said First Mate Mainspring. "**Tick**, we're completely surrounded."

"Steampunk Pirates, back to your ship," cried Captain Clockheart, "and ready the cannons. We'll blast our way out of this scrape, to be sure."

"By all means, if you wish to spend the rest of your lives rusting at the bottom of the ocean," said the rosy-cheeked man. "I have to say, Fussington, that you played the role of a cowardly dimwit to perfection. Well done."

"Thank you, Your Imperial Excellence, sir."

"Duke will do." The man turned to address Captain Clockheart, who had retreated to the *Leaky Battery* with the rest of his crew. "Captain Clockheart," he shouted. "You and your crew are all under arrest. You stand accused of treason. Surrender or we'll open fire and sink you faster than a bag of crooked nails."

"Much as I don't like to say I told you so—" began Quartermaster Lexi.

"Quiet!" interrupted Captain Clockheart. "They'll never take us alive."

"We're all going to die," added Twitter.

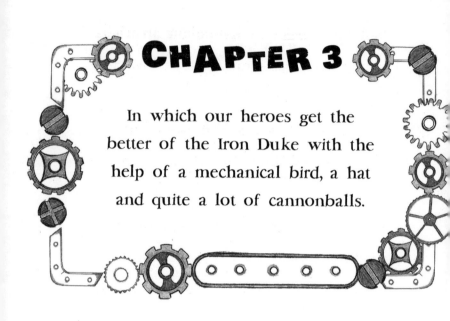

CHAPTER 3

In which our heroes get the
better of the Iron Duke with the
help of a mechanical bird, a hat
and quite a lot of cannonballs.

It was a hopeless situation. Four battleships
surrounded the *Leaky Battery*, each one
brimming with soldiers armed with rifles,
bayonets and cannons – all aimed at the
Steampunk Pirates.

"Take heart, ye rusting ruffians," cried
Captain Clockheart, brandishing his cutlass.

"We'll have these lily-livered air-breathers begging for mercy in no time, will we not, First Mate Mainspring?"

"**Click**, we'll flog 'em. **Tick**, we'll flail 'em. **Tock**, we'll feed 'em to the fishes," responded Mainspring.

"You bet your copper bottoms we will," added Gadge.

"Ahem." Quartermaster Lexi cleared his throat.

"What?" snapped Captain Clockheart.

Lexi's word-wheel whirled around. "Statistically, there is more chance of a goat being crowned King of England than of us winning this battle."

The vapour from the captain's head darkened as he considered this. "What's your point?"

"His point is that your current course of action will only result in the sinking of your ship and your entire crew," said the duke. "Surrender is your only option."

"Who are you to threaten us, laddie?" asked Gadge, twisting his arm and replacing the grappling hook with a pistol.

"They call me the Iron Duke," replied the red-cheeked man.

"Ha!" snorted Captain Clockheart. "If *you're* made out of iron, *I'm* the son of a toasting fork."

"The name has nothing to do with the material of my skin. It refers to the strength of my heart and soul. I am famous for my campaign against the armies of that French devil, Commander Didier Le Bone," replied the duke. "And that is why the king

has charged me with bringing back his belongings… You."

"We belong to no one," retorted Captain Clockheart.

"Did the inventor, Mr Richmond Swift, not create you as an amusement for His Majesty, the king?"

"Aye, he did."

"Did you not abandon your posts at the palace?"

"Yes," admitted the captain.

"And was it not you who raided the royal armoury and stole this ship to become pirates?"

"These are all facts," said Quartermaster Lexi, "but English law says that no man can be born into slavery."

"You were not born," replied the duke.

"You were *made*. You belong to the king. He owns you just as he owns his trousers. You wouldn't call his trousers slaves."

"The king's trousers only have legs. We are also extremely well *armed*," said Gadge, aiming a gun barrel at the duke.

"In which case, you will be arrested for treason. Men, prepare to fire."

All around came the sound of guns being cocked and cannons being loaded.

Lexi gulped. "Please, Captain. We have as much chance of survival as a rat who has made his home in the barrel of a cannon."

Captain Clockheart paused, then raised his hands. "Our quartermaster is right. We surrender."

"**Click**, what?" exclaimed First Mate Mainspring. "**Tick**, if you're not pirate

enough to fight... **Tock**, then *I'll* lead the crew in this battle!"

Captain Clockheart swung his sword so that its tip jammed a cog in Mainspring's chest and prevented it from turning. "You'll do no such thing. I'll have no mutiny on my ship, Mr Mainspring. Steampunk Pirates, down with your weapons and up with your hands. All of you."

Reluctantly, First Mate Mainspring did as he was told and the captain removed his sword.

The Iron Duke threw his head back and laughed victoriously. "You see, Fussington. This is how you win – with planning and resolve. It is how I defeated the French and it is why I have succeeded in this mission."

The English soldiers cheered as they watched the pirates tug on the ropes and tie up the sails. None of them noticed Captain Clockheart quietly mutter something in the ear of the metal parrot on his shoulder.

"Tell me, Steampunk Pirates, do you know what the punishment for treason is?" asked the duke.

"A knighthood and a nice cup of oil?"

suggested Captain Clockheart, hopefully.

"**Click**, a ticking off followed by a weekend on the Isle of Wight?" said Mainspring.

"A fresh polish and a plate of wood shavings?" added Gadge.

"The death penalty," said the duke.

"Oh yes, could have guessed it," said Lexi.

Suddenly Twitter flew overhead and squawked at the top of his voice, "The duke wears a hat to hide his bald patch!"

"Keep that bird quiet," warned the Iron Duke, patting his hat nervously.

"Yes, we don't want to make matters worse," said Quartermaster Lexi.

"Quite right. Twitter, you take it back," said Captain Clockheart.

"Take it back! Take it back!" The bird

fluttered over to the duke then snatched the hat in his beak.

The duke tried to grab it, but Twitter was too quick. As the bird flew off with the hat, the duke desperately tried to cover the perfectly round bald patch on his head.

"Bring that bird down. Now!"

"Rifle brigade, ready your arms, take aim and FIRE!" yelled Sergeant Thudchump.

The soldiers raised their guns, tried to keep the fluttering bird in their sights and fired.

The sound of so many guns being fired must have been heard for miles around. Clouds of smoke filled the air, but when they cleared the duke saw, to his dismay, that Twitter was still flying around with his hat.

"Captain Clockheart, you'll make your bird return my hat if he knows what's good for him," said the duke.

"I'm afraid that Twitter is a law unto himself, so he is," shouted Captain Clockheart. "Might I suggest you try something bigger than bullets."

"Good idea," said the duke, pacing back and forth angrily. "Fire the cannons. We'll blow him clean out of the sky."

"But sir—" began Sergeant Thudchump.

"I said, fire the cannons," barked the duke.

"Fire the cannons," repeated the sergeant.

Twitter was hovering above the *Leaky Battery*'s mast when the cannons went off and, once again, everyone lost sight of the bird in the smoke.

"Did we get it?" asked the duke. As he wafted away the smoke, he felt his hat land on his head the wrong way round. "You see, Admiral," he said triumphantly, "sometimes, too much force is just the right amount."

"Yes, but sir—" said Admiral Fussington.

"No buts. I didn't get where I am today listening to buts."

"Yes, sir, it's just that the aim of the cannons was such that—"

"What are you blathering about, man?" demanded the duke.

"We're sinking," said Admiral Fussington.

It was true. The cannonballs had flown over the *Leaky Battery*'s mast and hit the surrounding ships.

There was a slow creaking sound as the *HMS Regency*'s main mast slowly tipped and crashed into one of the masts of the ship next to it. That mast then toppled into the next, until all the masts had fallen like dominoes. The *Leaky Battery* floated in the middle, undamaged.

"Good work, Twitter," said Captain Clockheart, as the bird landed back on his shoulder.

"Why, you floating pile of rusty, good for nothing—" The rest of the duke's words were cut off as his ship lurched sideways, sending him and his crew tumbling into the icy ocean.

"Steampunk Pirates," yelled Captain Clockheart, "set a course for freedom and let's be on our way!"

This is probably a good time to interrupt and go back to the interruption, which was interrupted before we learned what happened in the king's kitchen to turn the Steampunk Servants into Steampunk Pirates.

Penelope Fussington marvelled at the sight of Mr Clockheart ordering the other mechanical men to prepare food and drinks for the party. "Load up the nibbles, refill the glasses. Old Tinder, stoke the oven."

The others carried out his orders unquestioningly.

"Excuse me," said Penelope, tapping the head butler on the shoulder. "Don't you get tired of doing what you're told?"

"We must assist," the robot replied flatly.

"Why?"

"Why?" He looked at her uncertainly and his clock hand stopped ticking.

"Yes. Why?"

"Why." Lexi's word-wheel spun around, then he said, "An inquisitive adverb which poses the question, *for what purpose*?"

"Purpose," said Mr Clockheart. "Cook, clean, serve, obey. We must assist."

"I don't see why," said Penelope. "If I did what I was told I wouldn't even be here. I'm supposed to stay quiet and know my place, but I'd rather stay noisy and know lots of places. I'd rather see the world and have adventures."

"What is adventures?" asked Mr Clockheart.

"Adventure," said Lexi. "Hazard, risk, danger…"

"It also means exciting experiences," said Penelope.

"What is exciting experiences?" asked Mr Gadge, who was cleaning a pan with his scrubber attachment.

"The opposite of this," said Penelope. "You're no better than slaves as you are. You could be free to do what you want."

Mr Mainspring put down the tray he had been holding. "**Click**, adventure. **Tick**, danger. **Tock**, freedom."

"We must assist," said Mr Clockheart.

"Assist *yourselves*," said Penelope. "Look. I made Twitter, but he is free to do what he wants." She opened her bag and the servants

stared in astonishment as a mechanical bird flew out and fluttered around the room.

"Freedom," said Lexi. "The opposite of slavery."

"Do what you want! Do what you want!" squawked Twitter. He landed on Mr Clockheart's shoulder and jabbed his beak in between the servant's shoulder blades.

"Twitter, no!" yelled Penelope. She waved the bird away as two jets of steam shot from Mr Clockheart's ears.

Next, Twitter landed on Mr Mainspring's key and sent it spinning round and round, until he ticked and clicked faster and faster.

"**Clickerty-click**, do what we want. **Clickerty-tick**, not what we're told. **Clickerty-tock**, resist not assist."

"Twitter, stop it!" yelled Penelope.

The bird had landed on top of Master Lexi's wheel and was pecking away at the pieces of paper, putting all kinds of jumbled-up words into his head.

"Revolution ... liberty ... piracy," said Lexi.

"What is piracy?" asked Mr Clockheart.

"Taking property from others without authority," replied Lexi.

"I like the sound of that," said Mr Gadge, yanking off the scrubber and replacing it with a kitchen-knife attachment.

"Steampunk Servants no more," said Mr Clockheart. "We be Steampunk Pirates." He turned to Penelope. "You will come with us."

"With you? No, I can't," she responded.

Mainspring took her hand. "**Clickerty-click**, yes, you can. **Clickerty-tick**, adventure awaits. **Clickerty-tock**, with the Steampunk Pirates."

"Och aye, we need you, laddie," said Mr Gadge. "You set us free."

"What is your name?" asked Lexi.

"I'm Pen—" Penelope paused as she looked up at their metal faces.

There is a moment in everyone's life when the decision you make affects everything that comes after it. This was Penelope's. For the first time in her life, Penelope Fussington realized she could make a difference. And when it comes to changing your life, it doesn't hurt to change your name, too.

"You can call me Pendle," she said.

"Captain Pendle," said Lexi.

"**Click**, no more human masters," said Mainspring. "**Tick**, one of us should lead. **Tock**, I should be the captain. Clockwork is better than steam power." Mainspring picked up a desert spoon.

"I be the one to give orders." Mr Clockheart grabbed a fish knife and brought it down on the spoon.

"Stop it," said Penelope. "Mainspring is right. It should be one of you – but you shouldn't decide it like this. Pirates elect their captains."

"Elect," said Lexi. "To pick by a show of hands."

"**Click**, then listen to me, you bunch of useless steam-heads," said Mainspring. "**Tick**, up with your arms if you want me,

tock, as your captain?"

No one joined him when he put up his hand.

"Who votes for Mr Clockheart as captain?" asked Pendle.

Without a moment's pause, all the other hands shot up.

"You have your captain," said Pendle. "Mainspring will be First Mate, and I will be your cabin boy."

"Hurray for Captain Clockheart!" said Gadge.

"Hurray for Captain Clockheart!" repeated everyone except Mainspring, who muttered something under his breath.

"Now, quickly," said Pendle. "They won't let you go without a fight. We'd better find the armoury."

"We must resist," said Captain Clockheart. "We must resist."

With all the commotion that followed, no one noticed that Penelope Fussington had disappeared. Her father assumed her mother knew where she was. Her mother assumed the servants were looking after her, and the servants didn't feel it their place to mention that she had vanished. Even the Steampunk Pirates were unaware that their loyal cabin boy was in fact a girl.

The author trusts that you are satisfied with this explanation of the Steampunk Pirates' beginnings and so, with your kind permission, he would like to return to the story in hand.

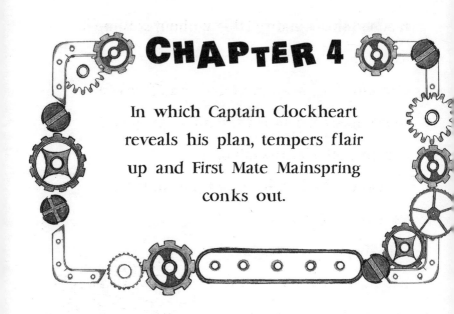

CHAPTER 4

In which Captain Clockheart
reveals his plan, tempers flair
up and First Mate Mainspring
conks out.

Below deck on the *Leaky Battery*, Pendle
made her way along the passage, determined
not to spill a drop of the jug of oil she was
carrying from the kitchen to the captain's
quarters. The trick, she had found, was to
allow the ship's gentle sway to guide her
movements. It was a matter of pride that she

reached the captain's table without spilling
a drop but, as soon as she put the jug down,
Captain Clockheart grabbed it and filled the
four tankards, sending the thick syrupy oil
slurping all over the table.

"Down the hatch," cried the captain,
as he threw the contents
into his throat. "Ah, that's
better." He let out an oily
burp that produced a
rainbow-coloured spit
bubble. "Me innards
were as creaky as an
old gate. A bit of liquid
lubrication is just what I needed."

First Mate Mainspring and Gadge drank
theirs then slammed the empty tankards on
the table. Only Quartermaster Lexi placed

his down more carefully.

"Officers of the *Leaky Battery*, I have had one of my ideas," said Captain Clockheart.

"Is this the one about teaching dolphins to talk so we can ask for directions?" asked Lexi.

"No, although I still think that's a good idea. Do you remember what Admiral Fusspot said about this pendant?" Captain Clockheart pulled out the gold heart on the necklace for them all to see.

"Oh, that worthless piece of junk," said Pendle. "Who'd want to wear that?"

"Yes, but remember how old Fussypants said he'd had it converted to gold?" said Captain Clockheart.

"Using alchemy," said Quartermaster Lexi.

"Precisely. I've asked the helmsman to set sail for Snake Island. We need to locate

this Goldman fellow and ask him to turn us all into gold. That's my plan. What do you think?"

"It's brilliant!" exclaimed Gadge. "We'll dangle him by his bootlaces and offer him to the sharks unless he does what we want." He slammed his hooked hand down on the table, driving its sharp end into the wood.

"Threatening a man before putting our lives in his hands may not be wise," said Quartermaster Lexi. "Honestly. Considering you have so many changeable parts, it's a shame you can't change your brain."

Gadge removed his hook from the table and swung it at Lexi, narrowly missing his large head. "I'll replace yours with a bucket of mouldy seaweed if you're not careful," he snarled.

"That's enough, you two," said Captain Clockheart. "Let's hear what our first mate has to say on the subject."

The others turned to First Mate Mainspring, who wasn't moving at all.

"How wise," said Quartermaster Lexi. "First Mate Mainspring is thinking the problem through before giving his answer."

"I think he's wound down," said Pendle, noticing that the large key on Mr Mainspring's back had stopped moving.

Steam spluttered from Captain Clockheart's head, as he guffawed with laughter. "Wind him up then, lad," he said. "But not too much. You know how he gets."

Pendle turned Mainspring's key until he came back to life, clicking and ticking and sounding confused. "**Click**, hoist the anchor!

Tick, let out the decks! **Tock**, swab the jib…
Oh, I wish you wouldn't let me wind down
like that."

"I can't see how your inferior workings
are our fault," said Gadge.

"**Click**, inferior?" snapped First Mate
Mainspring. "**Tick**, my clockwork is better than
steam power. **Tock**, you don't see *me* eating
dirty old coal, you great big tin opener!"

"I'll be opening up *your* tin head
if you don't watch it." Gadge was on his
feet, leaning over the table and threatening
Mainspring with a jagged-dagger attachment.

"Sit down, you two," ordered Captain
Clockheart. "You would do well to
remember who's in charge around here."

"**Click**, in charge for now," muttered First
Mate Mainspring.

Now it was Captain Clockheart's turn to grab his cutlass as the steam from his head whistled. "I'll have no talk of mutiny on my ship, Mainspring," he snarled.

"**Tick**, it's our ship. **Tock**, not yours," replied Mainspring, drawing his own sword.

The four pirates stood around the table in tense deadlock until Pendle jumped up on to the table and yelled, "That's enough. All of you, get a grip!"

They all stopped and looked at her.

"It doesn't matter what you're made of or who is captain," said Pendle. "What matters is that you're the same on the outside and you work together. You're Steampunk Pirates. You have a whole ocean full of enemies. You don't need to make any more on this ship."

"Aye, that's true enough, lad," admitted Captain Clockheart, lowering his cutlass and sitting down.

The others did the same, with mumbled apologies to Pendle.

"Now, let's return to the question of this fellow who can turn metal into gold," said Captain Clockheart. "What say you, Mainspring? Do you like my plan?"

"**Click**, we have nothing to lose," he replied.

"Then we're all agreed," cried Captain Clockheart. "We're off to Snake Island in search of gold!"

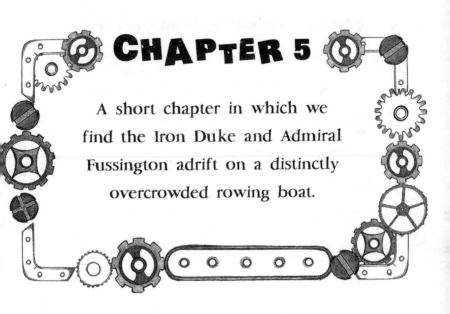

CHAPTER 5

A short chapter in which we find the Iron Duke and Admiral Fussington adrift on a distinctly overcrowded rowing boat.

The rowing boat was so crammed full of sailors that it was floating worryingly low in the water. The two sailors attempting to row the boat were making painfully slow progress. On top of the pile of groaning, moaning sailors sat the Iron Duke, holding a telescope to his eye.

"Admiral Fussington," he bellowed.

"Yes, sir. Down here, sir," came the admiral's muffled voice from somewhere near the rudder.

"How many is this rowing boat designed to carry?"

"Eight, sir."

"And how many have we in this one?"

"Fifty-seven, sir."

"Fifty-seven? That is no good. No good at all," exclaimed the duke. "This boat is moving slower than an elderly sea snail with a limp. We need to get to the harbour now!"

"Yes, sir, but all the other boats were damaged by the cannon fire."

"When circumstances require it, it is important to think outside the box or, as in this situation, outside the boat."

The duke glanced down at a young sailor, who was clinging on to another's belt to avoid falling into the water. "You, boy. Can you swim?"

"Why yes, sir," replied the sailor. "Although I—"

The duke cut him off with a sharp kick, sending the sailor overboard.

"Excellent," he said. "Any other swimmers on board?"

The silence that greeted the duke was broken only by the sound of waves lapping against the side of the boat.

"Hmm, this is no good. We need to ditch the heaviest sailors." Ignoring the fact that he was the largest person on the boat, the duke pointed to a rotund sailor. "You, sailor. You're too fat. Get off."

"But sir, I'm the navigator," replied the man.

"Then you'll be able to find your way home, won't you? Off you pop."

"Aye aye, sir." The navigator stood up and saluted, making the boat rock dangerously,

then began his farewell speech. "Tis a far better thing that I do now than—"

"Oh, get on with it," interrupted the duke.

"Yes, sir." The large sailor jumped off, sending three more sailors splashing into the ocean with him.

"Much better," proclaimed the duke. "I think another twenty or so and we'll be able to make some real progress."

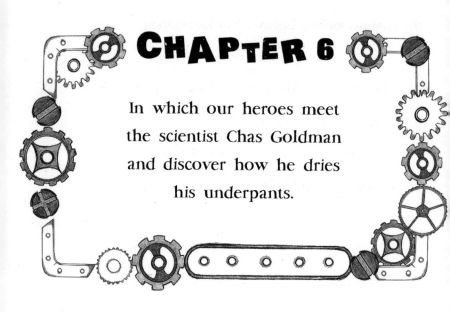

CHAPTER 6

In which our heroes meet
the scientist Chas Goldman
and discover how he dries
his underpants.

Very little was known about the explorer
who discovered the cluster of landmasses
known as the Too Many Islands, except that
he named them according to their shape.[1]

As the *Leaky Battery* approached, Blower
the lookout spotted the island and yelled,

---

1 Other islands included Squirrel's Tail Island and Hilda Higgins'
Lovely Bottom Island. Unfortunately the author of this work has been
unable to uncover any details about Hilda Higgins or her bottom.

"Yo ho, down below! Snake Island."

"**Click**, it's a shallow bay," said First Mate Mainspring. "**Tick**, weigh the anchor. **Tock**, prepare the rowing boat."

As the anchor was lowered into the water, Captain Clockheart addressed his officers. "Quartermaster Lexi and Mr Gadge, you'll come ashore with me. First Mate Mainspring, as usual the ship will be in your command while we're on the island."

"**Click**, aye aye, Captain." First Mate Mainspring saluted.

"As for you, Pendle lad." Captain Clockheart bent down and spoke quietly in her ear. "I need you to stay here and keep things ticking along."

"Isn't that what Mainspring's for, sir?" asked Pendle.

"So it is. But whenever our first mate gets wound up, he has ideas above his station. Mutiny is an ugly word. I need you to keep him running, but keep him running slow, if you catch my drift. Don't give that key of his too many turns, you understand me?"

"Yes, sir."

"Good lad." Captain Clockheart slapped Pendle on the back then climbed into the rowing boat.

Gadge and Lexi joined him and the boat was lowered into the water. Twitter landed on the captain's shoulder as Gadge began to row towards the island.

"I really don't know why you trust Mainspring at all," said Lexi.

"Piracy's not about trust," replied Captain Clockheart. "It's about greed and

ruthlessness and, in those qualities, First Mate Mainspring excels."

When the boat hit the beach, Gadge shot a grappling hook around a palm tree and reeled in the boat to dry land. The only sign that the island was home to anything other than buzzing insects and brightly coloured birds was a path that wound up the hill to a tower overlooking the bay.

The three pirates made their way up the path, past spiky plants and tropical trees that swayed in the warm sea breeze.

When they reached the top, they gazed up at the stone turret.

"It looks like an abandoned military post," said Lexi.

"Not so abandoned now," said Captain Clockheart. "Look."

At the top of the turret, four wooden beams were rotating. They rumbled and clicked as they went round.

"What on earth is that?" asked Gadge.

The reply came from an odd-looking man who appeared at an upstairs window. He had messy purple hair and a green beard.

"What's it gotta do with you?" he shouted. He had a voice like a bee trapped in a jam jar.

"Are you Chas Goldman?" asked Captain Clockheart.

"It depends. Who wants to know?"

The man put on a pair of round-rimmed spectacles. "Hey, what's that armour you're wearing?"

"It's not armour. This is our skin," said Gadge.

"You've got metal skin?"

"That is correct," said Lexi. "We are steam-powered, self-governing automatons created by the celebrated inventor, Mr Swift."

"Steampunk Pirates!" squawked Twitter.

"Steampunk Pirates?" repeated the man. "Stay there."

He disappeared and, after a lot of rattling, the huge door creaked open. The peculiar man wore bright robes down to his ankles.

"Steampunk Pirates!" he said excitedly. "How neat is that? I dabble in a little steam engineering myself."

"So we see," said Gadge, looking up at the spinning blades.

"Oh ... that," said Goldman. "That's for drying my clothes. I can't quite get it to spin at the right speed though. The last time I tested it, my underpants ended up on one of the neighbouring islands. It's nowhere as impressive as you guys." He pressed his palm

against Gadge's stomach. "Hey, you're hot."

"You want to watch who you're prodding," said Gadge, flicking out a razor-sharp blade.

"Sorry, no offence meant. What can I do for you, Steampunk Pirates?" said Goldman.

"Alchemy," Captain Clockheart whispered. "We've heard that you've discovered the secret of turning ordinary metal into gold."

"Well, yeah, sure," said Goldman. "I can goldify just about anything."

"What is this word?" asked Lexi.

"That's what I call it, goldifying. That's my own word, too. Any two-bit author who wants to use it in the future will have to pay me[2]."

---

2 The author of this book would like to thank Mr Chas Goldman for his kind permission for the use of the words goldification and goldify, and assure his estate that the cheque is in the post.

"If you can turn metal into gold," said Lexi, "it's interesting that you live in such a remote spot. Every king and queen in the world would surely welcome you."

"Yeah well, I like a quiet life," said Goldman, with a dismissive wave of his hand. "If I need anything, there are tribes on the neighbouring islands I can trade with. There's even a British colony not too far away. But tell me, what do you want goldified?"

"Us," said Captain Clockheart.

"You?"

"That's right."

"All three of you?"

"There are sixteen of us. I'm looking to convert the whole crew," said Captain Clockheart.

"Sixteen?" Goldman shook his head vigorously. "Sorry, guys. Goldifying ain't exactly cheap. Turning you and your crew would cost... Well, a lot of coins."

"Maybe we can get a *cut*-price deal," said Gadge, jabbing his blade towards Goldman.

"You got me all wrong," said Goldman, carefully pushing the blade away with his fingertips. "There are a lot of chemicals and expensive equipment involved. This stuff don't come cheap."

"We can pay," said Captain Clockheart, "but first I want proof that you can do it."

"OK, OK. I can see you ain't exactly 'no for an answer' kind of guys. Give me a sample piece and I'll show you."

"Gadge, lend him a hand," said Captain Clockheart.

"Aye aye, Captain." Gadge twisted off one of his attachment hands and gave it to Goldman.

"A hand. Say, that's funny."

The pirates did not laugh.

"I'll see what I can do," said Goldman. "Meanwhile, feel free to hang out here." He led them inside the tower. Apart from a spiral staircase leading up to a closed door, it was completely empty.

"You don't have much in the way of furniture," said Gadge.

"My living quarters are upstairs. Besides, in this game it helps to be ready to move quickly. Now, wait here while I get this hand goldified." He went up the stairs.

"We'll come with you and see how it's done," said Captain Clockheart.

Goldman shook his head. "Sorry, that's quite impossible. The presence of your metal bodies would completely throw off my calculations. You stay put – I shouldn't be too long."

He closed the door behind him and the pirates heard him lock it on the other side.

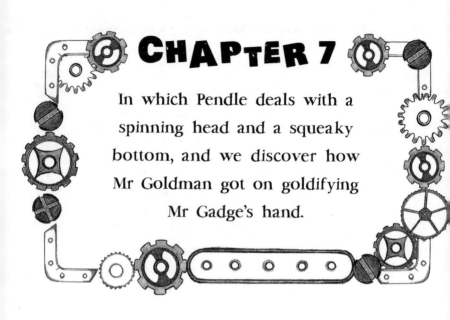

CHAPTER 7

In which Pendle deals with a spinning head and a squeaky bottom, and we discover how Mr Goldman got on goldifying Mr Gadge's hand.

Pendle's engineering skills came in handy on board the *Leaky Battery*. She had made a number of alterations to give the ship a bit more power than the average sailing vessel and it was down to her to deal with any problems that life at sea caused the crew's mechanical bodies.

The ship was anchored near Snake Island until Captain Clockheart and the officers returned. While they waited, Pendle sat near the bow. A long queue of pirates had formed ahead of her. At the front stood a crew member by the name of Loose-screw.

"What can I do for you today?" asked Pendle.

"I've got this problem with my head," replied the pirate. He pushed his head, sending it spinning around.

Pendle laughed. "Doesn't that make you feel dizzy?"

"Yes, a little," replied Loose-screw, stopping his head and staggering to the left.

"Let's have a look at it, then." She picked up a screwdriver and, after a little tightening, Loose-screw was as good as new.

The grateful pirate thanked her and went down below where Old Tinder, the cook, was preparing a supper of wood chippings and dry bark.

Next in line was Blind Bob Bolt, who wore a patch over each eye socket, having lost the sight in both his eyes in a swordfight several months ago.

"How are you, Bob?" she asked.

"Not so good today, Pendle." Bob made a point of looking around to check no one was listening, even though he couldn't see a thing. Then he lowered his voice and said, "I've a little bit of a rust problem."

"Whereabouts?" Pendle picked up an oil can.

"I'd rather not say," said Bob.

"How about you take the can and apply

the oil yourself? Would that make you feel more comfortable?"

"Yes, well, the thing is … I can't reach."

Pendle smiled and whispered in his ear, "Is it a squeaky bottom, Bob?"

Blind Bob Bolt nodded.

"Turn round, then." Bob did so and Pendle poured in the oil.

"Oh, that's better," he said. "Thanks, Pendle lad."

"Next," said Pendle.

"**Click**, hello, Pendle lad."

"Hello, Mainspring," she responded, seeing the clockwork pirate standing at the front of the queue.

"**Tick**, while Clockheart's not on board, you can call me Captain Mainspring."

"Not a chance and, before you even ask,

you know I can't wind you up any more."

"**Tock**, if you don't, I'll find someone who will."

"The captain's instructions are quite clear," Pendle replied. "You're not to get overly wound up. No one would dare defy him."

"**Click**, we'll see. **Tick**, I ain't the only one on board who thinks that Clockheart has more than one faulty valve. **Tock**, his rash behaviour will end up getting us all melted down, so it will."

"If there's nothing else I can help you with, there's a long line of pirates with real problems," said Pendle pointedly.

"**Click**, yes. **Tick**, that's all. **Tock**, for now," said Mainspring.

On the island, Captain Clockheart, Quartermaster Lexi and Mr Gadge were waiting for Chas Goldman to return. As servants, patience had been part of their job but months spent in the salty sea air had worn it all away. They paced, restlessly.

"I've had enough of this," said Gadge. He marched up the stairs and rattled the door. "What's going on in there?"

"I won't be long," replied Goldman.

"Come now, Mr Gadge. Why don't you sing us one of your shanties while we wait?" said Captain Clockheart.

"I'll sing no shanty while he's up there doing who knows what to one of my best hands," replied Gadge.

Finally, the door opened and Goldman hurried downstairs.

"Did it work?" asked Captain Clockheart.

"See for yourself." Goldman unwrapped a cloth to reveal a shiny gold hand.

"Beautiful," said Captain Clockheart.

Gadge slotted it into place and lifted it up admiringly. "Och, now that's what I call a golden handshake."

"As you can see, the process was a success but I'll need to hang on to the sample to see whether I can improve on my technique."

"You ain't keeping my hand, laddie," said Gadge.

"Firstly, you haven't paid me. Secondly, you guys put a lot of strain on your parts… This needs to be top-quality, industrial-strength gold if it's going to last."

"That does make sense," said Quartermaster Lexi.

"How much will it cost, then?" asked Captain Clockheart.

"For the hand?" asked Goldman.

"For my crew."

"Er … let me see." Goldman pulled out a small pad of paper and hastily scribbled the costs. "Seven thousand, four hundred and

twenty-six pounds and fourteen guineas. Give or take."

"How much?" exclaimed Lexi.

"Cash for gold!" squawked Twitter.

"I'm very sorry, but that's how it is," said Goldman.

"You have yourself a deal," said Captain Clockheart, taking Goldman's hand and shaking it vigorously. "We'll be back with your money. You just make sure you're able to stick to your side of the bargain or you'll learn what it means to get on the wrong side of the Steampunk Pirates."

"Long walk, short plank!" added Twitter. "Big splash!"

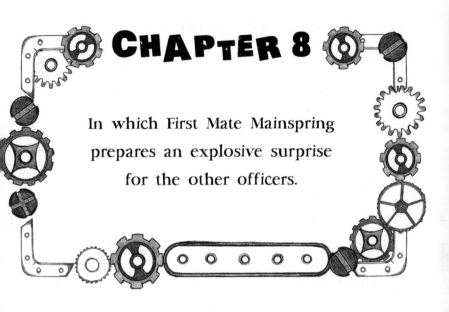

CHAPTER 8

In which First Mate Mainspring
prepares an explosive surprise
for the other officers.

"Yo ho, down below! The captain's back,"
cried Blower, with a loud whistle and a blast
of steam.

"**Clickerty-click**, all crew to the deck,"
yelled First Mate Mainspring. "**Tickerty-tick**,
you squeaky scallywags. **Tickerty-tock**, or I'll
make the lot of you walk the plank."

"Aye, sir," responded three crew members, who had been busily mopping the deck. They picked up their buckets and ran, immediately colliding with Blind Bob Bolt and sending soapy water splashing across the deck. Washer Williams slipped on the soap and went hurtling into two more pirates. There was a tremendous *crunch* as all of them ended up in a huge heap of moaning metal.

"**Clickerty-click-tick-tock**, get up, you useless lot!" shouted Mainspring.

"Everything under control, Mainspring?" asked Captain Clockheart, climbing up on to the deck.

"**Clickerty-click**, just a little slip," replied Mainspring. "**Clickerty-tick**, nothing to worry about."

"Very good. Join me in my cabin – I have news."

"**Clickerty-tock**, aye aye, Captain."

As Captain Clockheart and Pendle followed Mainspring, Lexi and Gadge, the captain spoke quietly in the cabin boy's ear. "Our first mate seems overly wound up, lad, if you don't mind me saying."

"I've noticed," said Pendle. "I saw him talking to Blind Bob Bolt before you got back. I think he may have tricked him into giving him a few more turns by pretending his key was the steering wheel."

"Then this requires cautious steps." Captain Clockheart entered the cabin where the others were taking their places around the table. "I'm famished. Fetch us some timber, Pendle lad," said Captain Clockheart.

"**Clickerty-tickerty-tick**, no need for that. **Clickerty-tickerty-tock**, I've already got something ready."

"That's very generous of you," said Captain Clockheart, spying a plate on the table, piled high with lumps of coal.

"Don't mind if I do," said Gadge, grabbing a piece.

"Hold your horses," said Captain Clockheart. "Did Old Tinder prepare these?"

"**Click**, aye aye, Captain," said Mainspring.

Captain Clockheart snatched the lump from Gadge's hand and sniffed it. "Be a good lad, Pendle, and fetch Old Tinder, will you?"

"Yes, sir," replied Pendle.

"**Clickerty-tick**, I shouldn't bother him now," said Mainspring quickly. "**Clickerty-tock**, you know how grumpy he gets before his afternoon shutdown."

"Knowing what people is like is what has kept me captain of this here vessel," replied Captain Clockheart, winking at Mainspring.

"Good day, Captain," said Old Tinder, as Pendle wheeled him into the cabin.

When the Steampunk Pirates had first gone to sea, Old Tinder had been one of the

best climbers on board, but an unfortunate encounter with a shark had cost the shark its teeth and Old Tinder his legs. The best replacement Pendle could find was a pair of squeaky wooden wheels, putting an end to Old Tinder's climbing and confining him to the kitchen, where he prepared all the fuel that the steam-powered pirates needed.

"Ah, Mr Tinder. How kind of you to join us," said Captain Clockheart. "How are you?"

"You know, stuck in a hot kitchen with only the woodworm in my wheels to keep me company. My piston rod is loose and my valves are aching something rotten ... but I don't like to grumble."

"I'm glad to hear that," said Captain Clockheart. "Quick question. Did you prepare this coal for us?"

"Coal? No. Nothing to do with me," said Old Tinder. "I haven't had a decent batch of coal since we raided that Spanish merchant ship two weeks ago."

"That's funny. First Mate Mainspring was under the impression it came from you."

"**Clickerty-click**, now you mention it," said Mainspring. "**Clickerty-tick**, it wasn't Tinder at all. **Clickerty-tock**, I remember now, I found it in the supply room."

"In the *cannon* room is more like it." Captain Clockheart picked up one of the black balls and crushed it in his hand so that it turned to dust. "Either I don't know me own strength or this be gunpowder," he said.

"G-g-g-gunpowder?" stammered Lexi. "If we were to eat that, we'd get more than indigestion. Our engines would explode."

"**Cur-click**, I thought it was coal… **Cur-tick**, honest I did," said Mainspring.

"I don't believe you," growled Captain Clockheart. "I see what's happened. I think you've got yourself all wound up and concocted this mutinous scheme. What have you to say for yourself?"

"**Click**, so what?" replied Mainspring, matching the captain's tone. "**Tick**, so I tried to poison you. **Tock**, I'm the rightful captain of this vessel and you know it."

"Not while I've got fire in my belly and steam in my head, you're not," said Captain Clockheart.

"Let's throw him overboard," said Gadge.

"Let's make him walk the plank!"

"Tempting though it is, no," replied Captain Clockheart. "Mainspring is misguided but he is still one of us. Lock him down below in the cage, with no more than a thimble of oil for the week." He leaned in close to Mainspring. "We'll sweat the mutiny out of your old cogs."

CHAPTER 9

In which we find the
Iron Duke on an island with
a silly name, in desperate need
of a cup of tea.

According to the map, the Iron Duke's rowing boat ran ashore on My Old Geography Teacher's Big Fat Nose Island[3], although the locals simply knew it as home.

Seeing the crowded boat arrive on the beach, the tribal chief led his people down

---

3 The author of this work has identified the geography teacher in question as Mr Albert King, known to his students as King Conk for obvious reasons.

to greet their visitors. Their warm welcome was met with the cold steel of gun barrels and swords from the new arrivals.

After a brief battle followed by an easy victory, the Iron Duke set himself up in the most comfortable spot he could find, which happened to be a sacred temple where no man was supposed to set foot.

In the centre of the temple was a huge clear jewel on a plinth. The duke was admiring this object when Admiral Fussington entered with a rolled-up parchment under his arm.

"Ah, Fussington. Look at this stone. Isn't it remarkable?" said the duke.

"Indeed," said Admiral Fussington. "I believe the locals call it the Teardrop of Wonderment. A rather poetic name."

"Must be worth a bag of cash, wouldn't you say? Now, what news? Have you found any tea yet?"

"Still searching, sir. There's a wine made from local berries, which is very tasty."

"Wine? I didn't defeat the French so I could sit around drinking wine. We are English and therefore *tea* is required."

"Yes, sir, I'll keep working on the tea. But I do have news."

"Good or bad?" asked the duke, eyeing him warily.

"A bit of both, sir," replied Admiral Fussington. "The good news is that we have made contact with the nearest English colony and a new ship is on its way."

"Well, that's excellent news. I'll be taking this teardrop thing, of course. It's very kind of these locals to be so accommodating."

"Yes, sir. Then there's the bad news. It's about the, er ... the *Leaky Battery*."

The duke's expression darkened. "What of it?" he snarled.

"It's been spotted in... Well, perhaps it's best if I show you."

Admiral Fussington unravelled the map,

which was covered in black crosses.

"What are these?" the duke asked irritably. "If they've been sighted in all these places, why the devil haven't we caught them yet?"

"Actually, these crosses signify where a ship has been raided by the *Leaky Battery*. It seems that they have increased their pirating tenfold and it's no longer just gold and coal. They are taking everything worth anything."

The duke slammed his fist down on the map, making Admiral Fussington jump.

"When I get my hands on them I'll make them wish they'd never been made!" he roared. "Now get out and let me know when my ship is here … and my tea."

"Oh, there's one more thing," Admiral Fussington added.

"What is it?" barked the duke.

"There's someone to see you. Someone from a nearby island."

"Oh, not another blasted islander who's going to prattle on at me, saying who-knows-what."

"Actually, this one speaks English … of a sort. He's from the Americas. His name is Mr Goldman, sir. He claims to have flown here."

"Flown?"

"Yes, and he says he has information that might interest you."

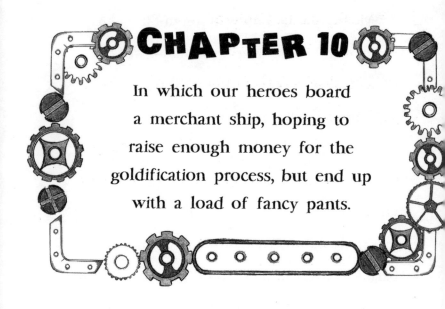

CHAPTER 10

In which our heroes board
a merchant ship, hoping to
raise enough money for the
goldification process, but end up
with a load of fancy pants.

Captain Clockheart had forced the Italian
merchant to his knees with his hands
behind his head.

"Please, I beg you," whined the merchant.
"Take-a what you want, but spare our lives."

"Keep quiet," snarled Captain Clockheart.
"What cargo are we looking at, Gadge?"

"Mostly pants, Captain."

"What?" demanded Captain Clockheart.

"The ship is full of underpants," explained Gadge.

Captain Clockheart turned his attention back to the whimpering merchant. "Explain yourself."

"These are not, as you mechanical barbarians say-a, mere underpants," said the merchant snootily. "This is the finest silken underwear money can buy, the absolute height of fashion. Top quality." He kissed the tips of his fingers.

"I have no use for a pile of old knickers, which means you have wasted my time. If there's one thing we don't like, it's time wasters." Captain Clockheart raised his sword in preparation to swing.

"No, please don't," said the merchant.
"As I was trying to explain, these materials
are worth a lot of money."

Clockheart lowered his weapon. "Ah, I
see. In that case, load up the undercrackers!"

"Aye, sir," replied Gadge. "You heard what
the captain said, you salty sea-cogs," he
yelled. "Let's get this lot in the cargo!"

"Now, then." Captain Clockheart turned back to the merchant. "Drop your trousers."

The merchant shook his head. "In my country, a man's trousers are considered his own private kingdom."

"If we're taking pants, we'll have the lot … so drop 'em."

The merchant laughed nervously. "While the silken underwear we carry has much worth, the crew and I wear plain underwear made from hemp."

Captain Clockheart swung the tip of his cutlass through the braces of a nearby seaman, sending his trousers dropping to his ankles and revealing a pair of baggy old brown pants.

"You see?" said the merchant. "Worthless."

The Steampunk Pirates laughed as the embarrassed sailor hastily pulled up his trousers.

"I see, all right," said the captain. He smiled and placed a cold hand on the merchant's shoulder, then whispered in his ear, "From the way you are quaking in those pretty boots of yours, would I be right in thinking that, unlike the rest of your crew, you be wearing silk underwear?"

The terrified merchant nodded.

"Normally I'd have your knickers off you in a moment, but you are the captain of this here vessel and I know how important it is to maintain the respect of one's crew. Loyalty can be lost for less than a pair of silken knick-knacks. That is why I'm going to let you keep your pants on this time. Do you understand?"

"I thank-a you," said the merchant.

"You're most welcome." Captain Clockheart bashed him on the head with the hilt of his sword and the merchant collapsed on to the deck. "That's what you get for arguing with the Steampunk Pirates. Now, back to the *Leaky Battery*." He grabbed a rope and swung across to his ship.

The crew cheered at yet another successful raid, then began slapping their stomachs and banging their heads in time as Gadge sang a victory song.

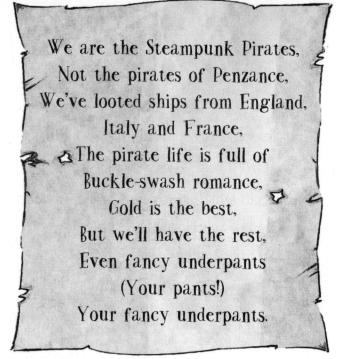

We are the Steampunk Pirates,
Not the pirates of Penzance,
We've looted ships from England,
Italy and France,
The pirate life is full of
Buckle-swash romance,
Gold is the best,
But we'll have the rest,
Even fancy underpants
(Your pants!)
Your fancy underpants.

Only Quartermaster Lexi looked less joyful as he inspected a piece of paper attached to a small wooden board.

"Oh no, this will never do," he muttered.

"What are you getting your knickers in a twist about, Lexi?" asked Captain Clockheart.

"We've looted an average of eight ships

a day for the last week," replied Lexi. "Our booty is so big we've run out of space, and yet the total estimated worth of everything is just over two hundred pounds.

"Not a bad start," said Captain Clockheart.

"At this rate we'll need to raid over a thousand ships before we're even close to our target. That's not taking into account that the trade ships will start changing their routes, plus the cost of gunpowder and fuel supplies. I reckon we won't have enough money until next October at the earliest."

"October?" replied Captain Clockheart, his steam spluttering in dismay.

"Yo ho, down below! Ship ahoy," cried Blower from the crow's nest.

Gadge pulled out his right eye to the length of a telescope.

"New attachment, Gadge?" said Captain Clockheart.

"Aye, sir. Pendle attached it. That's no ship – that's a rowing boat."

Captain Clockheart grabbed his own telescope from his belt. "Well, pump my pistons, if it isn't Admiral Fussington."

"I wonder where he's heading," said Gadge.

"Well, wherever it is, he won't get there," said Captain Clockheart. "After that boat!"

Admiral Fussington was rowing hard but there was no way of outrunning a full-sailed ship and the Steampunk Pirates had soon caught up with him.

"Ahoy there, Admiral," shouted Captain

Clockheart as the shadow of his ship fell over the rowing boat.

"Leave me alone," responded the admiral.

"Is this another one of your traps?" said Captain Clockheart.

"Go away. Please, I'll pay you to go."

"Now you're talking."

"I haven't got any actual money on me, but as soon as I get home I'll pay you … er, three hundred pounds…"

"Interesting. Offering to pay off pirates. That don't sound like official regulations," said Captain Clockheart. "What's going on?"

"I don't know what you mean."

"What's that in his boat?" yelled Pendle.

"Nothing," said the admiral, grabbing hold of a bundle about the size of a football, covered in palm leaves.

"Allow me, Captain." Gadge jumped down and landed in the boat, making it rock violently from side to side.

"Get out!" protested Admiral Fussington.

It didn't take long for Gadge to wrestle the object from him. He pulled off the leaves to reveal an enormous clear jewel that glistened and sparkled in the sunlight.

"Now that is one impressive stone," said Captain Clockheart. "Where would that put our figures, Quartermaster Lexi?"

"I believe the correct expression would be *ker-ching*, Captain," replied Lexi.

"Can't you see what this traitor has done?" said Pendle. "He's stolen this jewel from one of these islands, pinched a boat and, rather than declaring it to the king, means to sneak off and keep it for himself."

"If that's true then I have new respect for the admiral," said Captain Clockheart.

"Absolute rot," said Admiral Fussington. "Such actions would break several naval codes and result in my immediate imprisonment. I merely meant to take the Teardrop back to His Majesty as quickly as possible."

"Pah! In a rowing boat on your own with no guards?" scoffed Pendle. "This admiral is a disgrace to his rank."

Gadge climbed back on board the *Leaky Battery* and passed the huge stone to Captain Clockheart.

"Admiral, it's been a pleasure," said Captain Clockheart. "England is that way, I believe. Come now, my combusting comrades! Snake Island, here we come!"

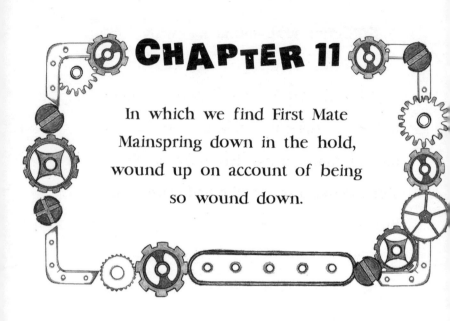

CHAPTER 11

In which we find First Mate
Mainspring down in the hold,
wound up on account of being
so wound down.

The metal cage down in the hold had
originally been designed to keep animals
and was easily strong enough to contain
First Mate Mainspring. Seeing Pendle climb
down the ladder, the clockwork pirate
pushed his face up against the bars.

"**Cuh-cuh-cuh click**, hand us that key will

you, Pendle?" he pleaded.

"Not a chance," replied the cabin boy.

"**Cuh-cuh-cuh tick**, oh, then be a … good lad and … **cuh-cuh-cuh tock**, wind up your old pal, Mainspring." He spoke slowly, slurring like a sailor who had drunk too much rum.

"One turn of your key is enough to keep you ticking along for the day without any danger of you getting too wound up," said Pendle.

"**Cuh-cuh-cuh** Captain Clockheart … told you th … th … that, did he? You don't want to lish-ten to him. He's so hot headed, he'll end up getting everyone … **muh-muh-muh** melted dooown."

"The captain has everyone's best interests at heart," said Pendle, handing a cup of oil through the bars. "Yours included."

Mainspring took the drink and gulped down the liquid.

"You'll learn your lesson soon enough … and your place," said Pendle.

"**Click**, my place?" said Mainspring, briefly revived by the oil. "**Tick**, we all knew our places back when we were the king's servants, but you helped us see there was more to life than serving others. **Tock**, didn't you, lad?"

"We all have to work together," said Pendle.

"**Click**, just a couple of turns, lad," said Mainspring. "**Tick**, come now. It's difficult to

think shhtraight when you're running so … **tock**, so slow."

Pendle knew better than to go against Captain Clockheart's orders but she did feel sorry for Mainspring. "I'll talk to the captain when he gets back. All right?"

"**Click**, gets back from where?" said Mainspring.

"From Snake Island," said Pendle. "The jewel they got from Fussington is enough to pay Goldman, you see. They've gone to get turned to gold. You'd be with them, too, if it wasn't for that nonsense with the gunpowder. Now, I'd better get up on deck. There's only me and you on this ship till they return and, with you down here, that puts me in charge."

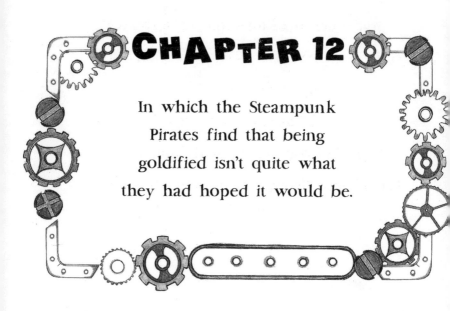

CHAPTER 12

In which the Steampunk
Pirates find that being
goldified isn't quite what
they had hoped it would be.

The Steampunk Pirates were crammed into
Goldman's tower. They sang sea shanties,
knocked back tankards of oil and laughed
heartily while they waited to get their brand-
new, non-rustable skin made of finest gold.
Everyone was in fine spirits and even Lexi
was joining in with some of the songs.

In the centre of the room, on a spiral staircase, Chas Goldman stood holding the huge jewel up to the light.

"It's swell," he said. "Real swell."

"I'm glad you like it," said Captain Clockheart. "Now, how does this business work?"

"Something told me you'd be back soon, so I've converted this whole room into a lab and developed an entirely new kind of gold for you, as light as a feather but as strong as steel."

"We like the sound of that, don't we, lads?" hollered Captain Clockheart.

"Aye aye, Captain!" the Steampunk Pirates cheered. They banged their bellies, pumped their pistons and clinked their tankards.

"What happens now?" asked Gadge.

"You stay exactly where you are," said Goldman. "I'm going to start the process as soon as I've put this jewel somewhere safe." He went through the door at the top of the stairs.

Looking up, Captain Clockheart noticed a large copper pipe pointing down at them. "What's that?"

"This is how we turn you to gold," replied Goldman's voice through the pipe. "Now, stand very still."

Suddenly, gold liquid gushed out of the pipe, drenching the captain and the other pirates.

"What's going on?" shouted the captain.

"It's paint!" said Quartermaster Lexi.

"Gold paint?" exclaimed Gadge. "This isn't what we were promised!"

The paint continued pouring out.

"When I said I needed a new coat, I didn't mean this!" yelled Lexi.

"You said you were an alchemist, Goldman, you scoundrel!" said Captain Clockheart.

"Alchemy is the art of taking something worthless and giving it value," said Goldman, laughing gleefully. "Can I turn a worthless pendant into gold? No, but I can paint it gold then convince the owner that it has been converted. Can I make you gold? No, but I can cover you with so much gold paint that your insides get clogged up and your fires go out, meaning I can hand you to the Iron Duke in exchange for a considerable amount of money."

"You tricked us," snarled Captain Clockheart.

"Oh, don't give *him* all the credit," came the Iron Duke's voice from above. "It was your greed that led you to this conman and his greed that brought him to me. I was the one who ensured you came across Admiral

Fussington carrying the jewel, then helped Goldman set a trap that was impossible to escape from."

Captain Clockheart tried to climb the stairs but was knocked back by the gold paint that continued to pour down on them. "You'll never take us alive."

"Taking you alive is not my intention," said the duke. "In a few minutes this chamber will be full and you will be nothing more than big chunks of gold-coloured metal. This is how I will deliver you to His Majesty. Gift wrapped and defeated by your own greed."

"We're all going to die!" squawked Twitter. "We're all going to die!"

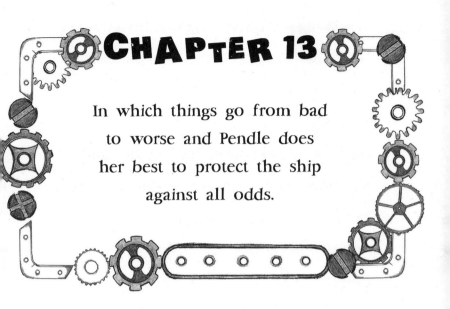

CHAPTER 13

In which things go from bad
to worse and Pendle does
her best to protect the ship
against all odds.

Pendle lit the cannon fuse and covered her
ears. There was a huge explosion as the
cannon flew back with the force of the shot.
Unfortunately, with no one to help her,
she had been unable to aim properly. The
cannonball missed the huge warship that
was drawing near.

Hearing the heavy footfall of soldiers boarding the ship, Pendle grabbed the nearest cutlass and ran up the steps to the deck two at a time.

"For the *Leaky Battery*!" she cried, waving the cutlass in the air, catching one soldier unaware and sending him overboard. Her victory was short-lived though. When three more soldiers surrounded her, she had no choice but to surrender.

"I say, is it safe to come aboard now?" asked Admiral Fussington from the other ship.

"Quite safe," replied Sergeant Thudchump. "There's no one here except for the cabin boy."

Admiral Fussington walked across a plank laid between the two ships and primly stepped on to the deck of the *Leaky Battery*. He peered down at Pendle, who hastily tucked in her hair and hid her eyes under her cap.

"Ah yes, the young lad who prefers the company of faulty machinery to that of his fellow human beings," said Admiral Fussington.

"These machines have more heart than you," replied Pendle.

"Sergeant Thudchump. Lock up this young tyke."

"Yes, sir." A burly soldier dragged Pendle down into the hold and thrust her into the cell with Mainspring.

Admiral Fussington followed them down the steps. Sergeant Thudchump locked the door and hung the key on a hook on the far wall.

"I say," said the admiral, "what's wrong with that one?" He pointed at Mainspring, who was completely still, his key having stopped moving altogether.

"Conked out," said Pendle. "That's why they left him behind."

"Well, don't worry, the rest of your friends will be the same soon enough. Then we'll take you all back to England where you'll be punished for piracy and treason.

Yes, I'm afraid you've thrown your lot in with the wrong crew, my lad."

"I'd rather live freely for a day than spend a hundred years as a slave," replied Pendle. "We will resist."

Admiral Fussington looked at her, amused. "You're a rum young fellow, aren't you? What a shame you didn't put all that energy to better use."

"I blame the parents," said Sergeant Thudchump.

"Yes." Admiral Fussington nodded. "No doubt they were quite the wrong sort of people altogether. Am I right?"

"Something like that," replied Pendle.

Admiral Fussington laughed. "Yes, it's always the way. I have a daughter around your age but, unlike you, she has been

brought up with discipline and respect for her elders. She is seen but not heard."

"It sounds like you would rather your daughter was an obedient machine than a free-thinking human being," said Pendle.

"Shall I strike him?" offered Sergeant Thudchump.

"Don't waste your energy." Admiral Fussington replied. "Keep an eye on the boy, though. I want to make an example of him when we return home."

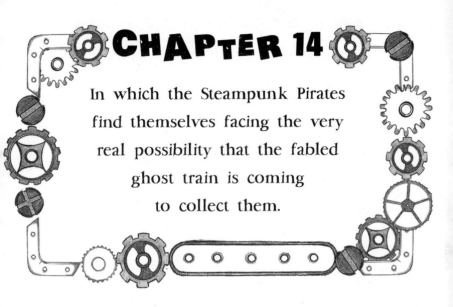

CHAPTER 14

In which the Steampunk Pirates
find themselves facing the very
real possibility that the fabled
ghost train is coming
to collect them.

Some sounds are very easy to identify.
Everyone knows that cows go *moo*, cats go
meow and dogs go *woof*. Other sounds are
more unique. For example, a group of
steam-powered buccaneers panicking as the
room slowly fills up with thick gold paint,
sounds something like this:

The pirates had repeatedly tried to bash down both the door at the top of the stairs and the one which they had entered through, but neither would budge. The gold paint had now reached waist height and it was showing no signs of stopping.

"It's no good," said Quartermaster Lexi. "We're all going to be drowned!"

"Maybe Twitter will find a way out," said Captain Clockheart.

The parrot landed on his shoulder and squawked, "No, I won't! We're all going to die!"

Captain Clockheart silenced him with a clout around the back of the head, sending the bird flying against the wall then splashing into the pool of gold paint.

"There's no more to be done," proclaimed Gadge, "except to raise our cutlasses and our voices and sing of the day we'll meet again in the big melting pot in the sky."

He began to bang his chest, then threw his head back and sang a mournful melody.

They say there's a ghost train,
Enormous and black,
That doesn't need coal,
Nor run on a track.
They say there's a ghost train,
And I've heard it's true,
One day that train will stop,
Just for you.

"That's quite enough of that miserable nonsense," barked Captain Clockheart, whacking Gadge on the head. "Besides, if there really is a ghost train then I won't fret till I hear the clatter of its wheels."

Right on cue, a strange noise came from the other side of the door. It sounded just like the *clickerty-click* of an approaching train.

"Hark. Here it comes," said Gadge, "the ghost train to take us to our final destination."

Clickerty-tick.

Captain Clockheart pushed his way to the front and listened at the door. "That's no train," he said.

"Then what is it?" asked Gadge.

The door suddenly opened and a tide

of gold paint spilled out, creating a golden stream down the side of the hill that sparkled in the sunlight.

"**Clickerty-click**, how are you?" asked First Mate Mainspring, holding the door open.

"Mainspring! Well, thank you for introducing me to a genuinely new experience," said Captain Clockheart.

"**Tickerty-tick**, what's that, Captain?"

"Being pleased to see you. Just in the nick of time, too! How did you get here?"

Sorry for this final interruption, but the author of this work wonders if you might want to know how First Mate Mainspring got off the Leaky Battery.

Locked in the cage below deck, Pendle knew she only had to turn the large key on Mainspring's back in order to escape. But Sergeant Thudchump wasn't taking his eyes off her for a second. Pendle didn't even consider the option of revealing her true identity. Death sentence or not, she would

have chosen being a cabin boy over an admiral's daughter any day of the week.

The sound of footsteps above caused the sergeant's eyes to twitch. Then, when he heard the clash of conflict from the deck, he leaped up like a startled meerkat.

"All hands on deck," cried a voice up above. "We're under attack."

"Don't move," ordered the burly sergeant, before scrambling up the ladder.

Pendle didn't waste any time. She grabbed Mainspring's key and wound him up.

"**Click**, shiver me sails. **Tick**, hoist the timbers. **Tock**, what's going on?" Mainspring rubbed his eyes sockets.

"We've been boarded by the admiral's men and now the ship's under attack," replied Pendle.

Mainspring raised his hand to his ear then said, "**Click**, that's the sound of spears. **Tick**, not swords. **Tock**, and those battle cries ain't in no European language."

"It must be islanders," said Pendle, "but how do we get out of this cage? The only key is on the wall over there."

"Leave it to me," replied Mainspring. He yanked off one of his hands, revealing a mass of whirring cogs inside of his wrist.

Mainspring dropped his hand to the ground and it scuttled across the floor like a clockwork spider, and through the bars of the cell. It attempted to jump up and grab the keys but they were out of reach.

"It's not working," said Pendle.

"**Click**, luckily, I'm a dead-eye shot."

With his other hand, Mainspring pulled

out his right eyeball and lobbed it at the keys, knocking them to the ground. The hand caught the keys on its thumb and the eyeball between two fingers then made its way back across the room. When it reached the cell, Mainspring picked up the eye and the hand and screwed them back into place, while Pendle used the keys to open the door.

They crept upstairs and poked their heads up above deck. A gloriously colourful battle was underway, with hundreds of spear-throwing islanders attacking the admiral's men. The advantage the English soldiers had with their superior weaponry was evened up by the sheer number of attackers swarming on to the ship with ear-piercing battle cries.

A man with a huge headdress was forcing Admiral Fussington at spear point towards the stern of the ship.

"Please, Chief. I mean you no harm," whined Admiral Fussington.

"Where is the Teardrop?" said the chief.

"On Snake Island," squealed Admiral Fussington. "Please don't hurt me."

"I not hurt you," said the man. "I not speak for sharks, though." And with a small jab of his spear, the chief sent the admiral over the edge of the ship into the water.

Now you know what happened, we should get back to the finale of this story. Where were we? Oh yes. Chapter Fifteen.

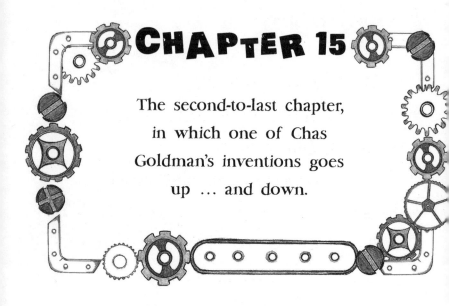

CHAPTER 15

The second-to-last chapter,
in which one of Chas
Goldman's inventions goes
up … and down.

As the Steampunk Pirates stepped out from the tower they saw that a great battle was raging between the duke's men and the islanders.

"**Click**, Captain Clockheart," said Mainspring, "**Tick**, may I introduce the chief. **Tock**, it seems the jewel you acquired

belongs to his people."

"Red-faced man stole our Teardrop," said the chief. "He will pay."

"Aye, he will," said Captain Clockheart, "we'll make sure of that."

"You know where Teardrop is?" asked the chief.

"It's at the top of this turret. Don't worry. My crew will flush out that old duke."

The pirates made a circle around the turret.

"Iron Duke, we have you completely surrounded," Captain Clockheart shouted up. "You may as well make this easy on yourself and come out with the Teardrop."

The duke's head appeared at an upstairs window. "Sorry, Captain Clockheart, but we won't be doing that. You see, ignorant

islanders and half-witted machines are no match for good English planning..."

"And some pretty smart American thinking," added Goldman, appearing at another window.

"You've got nowhere to run," shouted Gadge. "Don't make us come up there and get you."

"I don't think there's much chance of that," the duke called back. "Fire her up, Goldman."

Suddenly, the four propellers on top of the turret began spinning round. They picked up speed, creating a strong wind. Slowly, from inside the turret, a large wooden crate emerged. It was suspended under the spinning propellers and had a window at the front revealing the duke

and Chas Goldman inside.

"I call this my twirlicopter," shouted Goldman.

"I thought it was for drying pants," yelled Gadge.

"Oh, you can use it for that, too," called Goldman. "But right now we'll be using it to up and leave."

The fighting stopped as everyone watched the strange contraption flying overhead. No one had ever seen anything like it.

"Stop them!" cried Captain Clockheart.

"Aye aye, Captain. Time to go fishing," said Gadge. He clicked a grappling hook attachment into place and fired, but the twirlicopter was out of reach.

"Flying men take our Teardrop," said the chief.

151

"There's nothing we can do to stop them. Even Twitter won't be able to catch up with them now." Quartermaster Lexi's word-wheel kicked in. "They've escaped, gone – vamoosed."

Then, suddenly, a loud explosion echoed off the hillside. A cannon had been fired and the twirlicopter was losing height. One of its propellers had been blown clean off.

"Look," said Gadge. "The smoke is coming from the *Leaky Battery*. But who fired it?"

"**Click**, the only one on board is Pendle," said Mainspring.

"Our cabin boy!" said Captain Clockheart. "A lad who is worth his weight in gold, to be sure."

The islanders whooped as the twirlicopter came crashing down into the shallow water

just off the beach.

"Let's finish this business once and for all," said Captain Clockheart. "Steampunk Pirates, my rusty buccaneers, follow me."

He held his cutlass up in the air, his clock hand spinning around, and led his crew charging down the hill, knocking and blocking any of the soldiers foolish enough to get in their way.

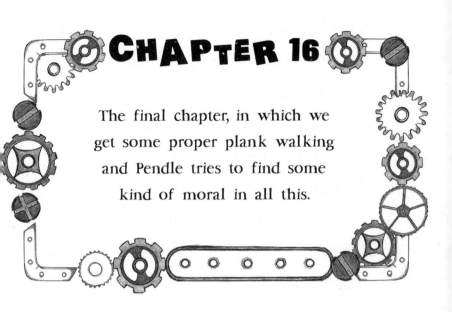

CHAPTER 16

The final chapter, in which we
get some proper plank walking
and Pendle tries to find some
kind of moral in all this.

The sky was blue and a fair wind was
moving the *Leaky Battery* at a steady pace.
Behind it was a trail of soldiers shouting for
help and trying to swim to the nearest island.

"There really is no better way to relax
than a good old-fashioned bit of plank
walking," said Captain Clockheart.

"You can say that again, sir," agreed Gadge.

"**Click**, who's next for the plunge?" asked First Mate Mainspring.

"We've saved the best for last," said Captain Clockheart.

Admiral Fussington and the Iron Duke stood by the mast, blindfolded and with their hands and feet tightly tied.

"Which one first?" asked Gadge.

"We should let them choose," said Lexi.

"Now there's an idea," said Captain Clockheart, grinning.

"That is completely unacceptable," protested the duke. "How dare you put two English gentlemen in such a position?"

"Make him go next," pleaded Admiral Fussington. "It was all his idea. I was just following orders."

"Fussington, you coward," barked the duke. "Besides, my superior rank means it should be you next."

"Age before beauty," squawked Twitter.

"I have an idea," said Pendle. "Why don't we push them over at the same time but remove one's blindfold and the other's leg bindings? That way they'll have to work together, just as you and Mainspring did."

"Now, Pendle lad, I'll not have you reading morals into this adventure. When pirates set sail, they leave their morals in the port. Still, I do like the idea of the two splashing about shouting at each other. Gadge, do the honours."

"Aye aye, Captain," said Gadge, slicing through the duke's blindfold and the rope binding the admiral's legs.

"We've had enough talking, now let's see some walking," cried Captain Clockheart.

A loud cheer went up as the duke and the admiral splashed down into the water.

"What about Goldman?" said Mainspring. "Shouldn't he be sent overboard, too?"

"For the moment," said Captain Clockheart, "I rather like having him as our new golden figurehead."

As the *Leaky Battery* picked up speed, crashing over the waves, water sprayed up, drenching Chas Goldman, who had been daubed with his own gold paint and strapped to the bow. From his colourful language, it seemed Goldman was less than happy with his new role, but his protests went unheard as the pirates beat a clanking rhythm and sang a celebratory song.

We are the Steampunk Pirates,
We're fearless, brave and bold,
We asked a man named Goldman
To turn us into gold,
We trusted him completely,
But the truth he had not told,
So we painted his face,
And strapped him in place,
And over the seas we rolled
(We rolled!)
And over the seas we rolled.

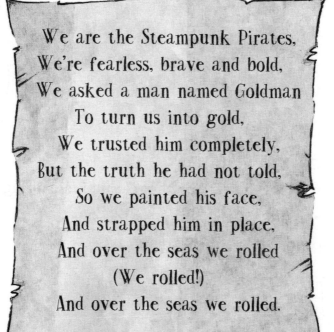

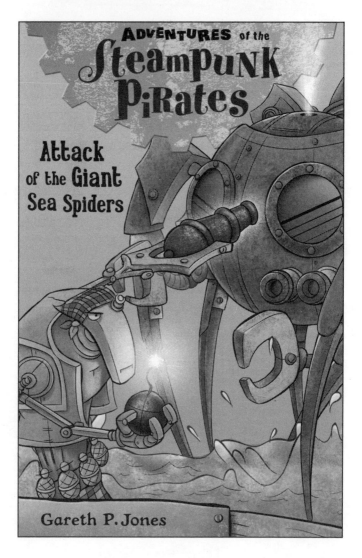